TWISTER

Andrew Fusek Peters
and Polly Peters

Evans

PLAYS WITH ATTITUDE

To find out more about the authors, visit www.tallpoet.com

Published in 2007 by
Evans Brothers Ltd
2A Portman Mansions
Chiltern Street
London W1U 6NR

Reprinted 2010

The right of Andrew Fusek Peters and Polly Peters
to be identified as the authors of this Work has been
asserted by them in accordance with the Copyright,
Designs and Patents Act 1988.

Any performance or rehearsal of this play must be given under
licence. All licence applications should be sent to: The Rights
Department, Evans Publishing Group, 2A Portman Mansions,
Chiltern Street, London W1U 6NR.

British Library Cataloguing in Publication Data

Peters, Andrew (Andrew Fusek)
    Twisted. - (Plays with attitude)
    1. Bullying - Juvenile drama 2. Children's plays, English
    I. Title II. Peters, Polly
    822.9'14

ISBN 9780237533731

Editor: Su Swallow
Designer: Robert Walster, Big Blu Design
Printed in Malta

Cover image istockphoto.com

FOREWORD

Twisted explores themes of bullying, peer pressure, family relationships and self-worth. The play begins with one known fact – Gretel is in a coma. The central question throughout is – what actually happened? In the course of finding an answer, the story unfolds through flashback, the reactions of those around her, speculation and visual dramatic devices. The play also addresses a second, more subtle question – what motivates someone to become a bully? At the end, when the audience is invited to consider who caused Gretel's coma, the answer is not as clear-cut as might be expected.

This play requires a minimum cast of 17, but is also designed for a much larger cast. *Twisted* presents a mix of psychological realism, stylization, ensemble performance, monologue and improvisation. The inclusion of directions for some improvised scenes is to allow opportunities for imaginative development of the text and to offer hands-on ownership by the cast of sections of the performance. Alternatively, these scenes can be used for extension script-writing by pupils. *Twisted* can be used for a full-length performance, or individual scenes can be explored practically during drama lessons or youth theatre sessions. Sections could also be used for discussion in English and in PHSE. *Plays with Attitude* have been written to appeal to KS3 and 4 performers and audiences. They offer a text-based framework for developing the individual and ensemble-based performance skills explored by students through class-based improvisation.

Set requirements are basic: chairs of different types and a white screen. The emphasis is on maintaining a fast pace and smooth transition between scenes, hence the limited set changes. Lighting should portray the different locations.

CAST LIST

GRETEL'S FAMILY:
GRETEL
MUM: Margaret
DAD: Walter
SIMON
GEORGE

GRETEL'S FRIENDS:
ROWAN
SAM
OLLY
HAZEL
CINDY

MADDY'S GANG:
MADDY
HOLLY
IVY
JO
LORRAINE

PC MIDDLETON
WPC RILEY

JOHN: Gretel's boyfriend
CHRIS: Party host
PARTYGOERS: six speaking roles
DOCTOR

Scene One

Blackout. Whole cast ranged around stage, backs to audience, holding individual static poses. Lights up slowly.

ALL: [*Whisper*] Have you heard?

Chorus whisper creates eerie echo effect. One by one, performers turn, asking out loud, Have you heard? *which gives the cumulative effect of a Chinese whisper. After each has turned, resume different static poses and continue the whisper until all face audience*

ALL: What?

Cast moves rhythmically around stage, repeating individual lines to each other as they pass. Voices build as the lines begin to cut across each other simultaneously

1:        She's in hospital.

2:        The ambulance came.

3:        What happened?

4:        She was so pale.

5:        Who found her?

6:        It was awful.

7:        They put her on a stretcher.

8:        Did you know her?

9:        It was dark.

10:       Where was she?

11:       No-one saw anything.

ALL: Anything.

12:       There must have been someone else!

13:       She was alone when she was found.

14:       Lying there.

15:       She's in a coma.

16:       Lying there.

Lone voice shouts

1:        So what the hell happened?

All silent, turn to stare. Exit

Scene 2

Gretel, spotlit, wearing hospital gown. Sound effects during monologue of distant voices and hospital equipment.

GRETEL: It grows light then dark and there are sounds I think I ought to know, but can't quite place - strange birds; scuffling in the dark. The trees are close overhead and it's hard to see the path or even feel my feet. Such soft pine needles: swallow sound; deaden every step. In the silence, I hear the leaves whispering behind my back 'Abandoned...been abandoned!' Over and over. I thought this was the way home but now I'm no longer sure. Nothing looks familiar. No comforting white pebbles to mark the way, no friendly dove to greet or guide me. And you know, I can't tell if it's me moving through the trees or the trees moving through me. *[Sings]* 'If you go down to the woods today, you're sure of a big surprise. If you go down to the woods today, you'd better go in disguise...' How does it go? Even the tune is lost. Can't remember. I'm so tired, so sleepy, I just want to go home. [*Jerks awake as if from a dream and sobs*] Mummy? I want my Mummy. It's getting dark again. Don't leave me. Mu-m-my...

Blackout. Exit

Scene 3

Three groups are on stage: Family, Friends and Maddy's gang, each in still tableau. When one group is performing, the other two remain in a frozen position until it is their turn. Mum and Dad are seated, watching audience as though they are the TV.

MUM: What's the time?

DAD: [*Watching TV. Ignores her*] There's the clock.

MUM: [*Glancing upwards*] Oh. Twenty past ten. Think I'll head up soon. Did they all take keys with them?

DAD: What? How should I know? Check if you're fussed. But you won't catch me getting out of bed for anyone.

Sound of door slamming

MUM: That'll be Simon.

DAD: One down, two to go. [*Ignores Simon as he enters*]

SIMON: Hi Mum, anything to eat?

MUM: Of course love. There's a pork pie in the fridge, but leave some for Georgie.

SIMON: George, Mum. He hates being called Georgie, remember? Says it makes him sound like a girl.

DAD: *[Doesn't look up]* And you'd know all about that, wouldn't you?

MUM: Walter! Please...*[She falters and turns back to Simon]* Anyway, to me you're all still my babies. Time goes so quickly, it's hard to remember you're nearly grown up.

DAD: God, listen to you! You'd have 'em back in nappies, soft cow. Grown up is good. Grown up is earning their own way, not sponging off us, isn't it twinkle toes? *[To Simon]* Well? Or has our little dancing dream still not got any ideas about what he'll do next year?

SIMON: We get all that stuff at school, Dad: careers and further education and stuff.

DAD: Ah! 'Careers' is it? 'Job' not good enough? Well, I've had a job since I was sixteen. Timber yard's always been good enough for me. Good enough for George too, so it should damn well be good enough for you. Unless you're thinking of dancing and prancing your way to glory? Eh?

SIMON: *[Quietly]* It's lessons, Dad, that's all.

DAD: Lessons? You don't get enough of those in school then? What's it called then, these 'lessons'?

MUM: You know what it's called, Walter.

DAD: And I'm asking again. I'm interested.

SIMON: *[Resigned]* Contemporary Dance.

DAD: Con-temp-or-rary! What the hell does that mean?

MUM: Oh, Walter...

DAD: Will you STOP 'Waltering' me? [*To Simon*] Well?

SIMON: I just like it, that's all. And I'm good at it. It's only a hobby.

DAD: Do you think they checked him over properly when he was born, eh? 'It's another son Mr Ashwell.' Daughter, more like. Eh?

Moment of tense silence. Door slams. George enters

GEORGE: Hi...[*Looks around*] What?

MUM: Nothing.

DAD: Good night was it? You're back early. Not even chucking out time yet.

GEORGE: Oh, yeah. The lads went on to some club in town. Didn't fancy it. Anyway, said I'd go in for the early delivery at the yard in the morning. Don't want to be too shattered for that.

DAD: Good lad. Good to see that some people have got their priorities straight.

GEORGE: [*Yawning*] Right. Where's Gretel?

DAD: No idea. Ask your mother.

MUM: Oh. Er, party at Chris's house. Parents are away for the night…

DAD: What? And do they know about this party? Christ, if any of you tried that on while we were out…

GEORGE: Any food Mum? I'm starving.

MUM: There's a pork pie in the fridge for you and Simon to share.

GEORGE: Great! [*To Simon*] Come on.

Doorbell rings

DAD: I knew it! She hasn't got her keys, has she? Leave her there for a bit.

SIMON: I'll go.

GEORGE: *[Glances at Dad]* It's all right. I will. *[Exits]*

Muffled voices offstage

DAD: Stupid girl. We should get a pair of keys tattooed on her forehead. She spends enough time looking in the mirror. Then she'd remember, eh?

Two PCs enter

GEORGE: Mum…Dad…it's the police.

POLICE 1: *[Holds up warrant card]* I'm PC Bob Middleton, Mrs Ashwell, Mr Ashwell, and this is WPC Linda Riley.

MUM: What?

POLICE 2: You are the parents of Gretel Ashwell?

DAD: Yes. What's she been up to? Has she been arrested? I'll kill her…

POLICE 1: No sir, nothing like that. I'm afraid to tell you, she's been admitted to hospital.

MUM: But…What?…What's happened?

Group freezes. Gretel's friends spotlit, consoling each other. There are silences between the lines where they struggle for words

ROWAN: I just can't believe it.

SAM: Nor me.

OLLY: It's awful.

ROWAN: I mean…she was just lying there.

HAZEL: And she was so pale, like she had no blood in her.

SAM: I was afraid they wouldn't find a pulse.

OLLY: Awful.

ROWAN: Did you touch her?

OLLY: No! What if she hadn't been warm? And anyway, they always say not to move people, don't they?

SAM: I wish we'd seen…I mean we still don't even know…

HAZEL: Did the paramedics say anything?

SAM: Don't think so, just that she was unconscious.

OLLY: Oh God!

SAM: I know, I know.

ROWAN: If only one of us had been with her.

HAZEL: I know, I keep thinking that too. If only we'd seen what happened.

SAM: Well, someone must have. I mean come on, a whole partyful of people? She can't have been the only one outside, she just can't!

OLLY: Awful. Awful. D'you think she's in the hospital yet?

ROWAN: [Hugging Cindy] Oh Cindy, you look just like I feel.

CINDY: Yeah, awful.

Friends' group freeze. Maddy's gang spotlit

HOLLY: One less geek then! Have you seen the rest of them?

IVY: [Giggling] Yeah, the freaks! Geeky girlies. [Sarcastic] Aaah!

JO: Their 'ickle fwiend got hurted. Diddums.

MADDY: So it seems.

LORRAINE: [Simpers]Little Miss 'Here's my homework, Mr Simpson. I stayed up all night to finish it on time'. [Makes gagging motion]

JO: Miss 'Would you like to borrow my Classic FM CD? I listen to it loads!'

LORRAINE: Did you see all the fuss? Ambulance and all. It's just gone.

MADDY: Like I care.

HOLLY: Silly cow.

IVY: Had it coming.

HOLLY: That'll be her second 'unfortunate' accident then. The first was being born!

Gang freeze. Friends' group spotlit

ROWAN: Where's John? Why wasn't he with her?

OLLY: Dunno. I'm sure they were together earlier.

SAM: They were in the kitchen soon after we arrived. Haven't seen him since. Come to think of it, don't think I saw Gretel after that.

ROWAN: What were they doing?

SAM: Just talking. I wasn't looking that closely. I think they were both looking a bit, sort of, serious. But, like I said, I wasn't exactly filming the moment.

OLLY: What about the Hell-hags?

HAZEL: Huh. Her bitchiness the queen: Maddy and her snide-as-dyed peroxide crew? Couldn't exactly avoid them.

OLLY: I mean...Do you reckon they...?

HAZEL: They're capable of anything...gum-chewing, bottle-swigging, fag-puffing...*[Grimaces and turns to Cindy]* Didn't they have a go at you, earlier? *[Cindy nods]*

SAM: Nasty bits of work. So listen, I know it's not exactly the moment but I overheard something fantastically vicious about Maddy. Can't wait to spread it…

ROWAN: Not now Sam. What about Gretel?

CINDY: Yes. Gretel.

Friends freeze. Maddy's gang spotlit

JO: Attention-seeking, stuck-up little…

HOLLY: Well, she's got all the attention she wants now, eh Maddy?

MADDY: I'm bored.

IVY: Oh. Sure. Show's over.

LORRAINE: She'll be all right though, won't she?

MADDY: Of course she will.

IVY: What d'you reckon? She was pretending? Playacting?

MADDY: Yeah.

Gang freezes. Gretel's family and police spotlit

DAD: What do you mean, you 'don't know anything for certain'? Is there something you're not telling us?

MUM: Which hospital? When? I mean…why? Oh God, what's wrong with her? What?…What do we…?

POLICE 1: Perhaps you'd both like to sit down.

DAD: Sit down? Sit down! Is that the best you can offer? I want answers, not mollycoddling.

GEORGE: Steady on.

SIMON: All right, Mum. *[Puts his arm around her]*

MUM: What…what can you tell us?

POLICE 2: Well, Mrs Ashwell, it seems that an ambulance was called to an address in Oakley Road, where your daughter was found unconscious…

MUM: Oh…

DAD: Unconscious! Had she been drinking?

MUM: Walter!

DAD: Well, had she?

POLICE 1: We don't know sir. They'll assess her at the hospital, we should know some more after that.

MUM: *[Dazed]* The hospital…St Mary's, yes?

PC nods

So, so we need to go there right away…um, car keys?…handbag?…take things…do we need take things for her? My baby. My little girl. Please, don't let it be serious.

POLICE 2: Would you like us to drive you there or…?

DAD: No, I'll get the car.

POLICE 1: I'm afraid there are some questions we'll need to ask you, but we'll wait until you've seen your daughter.

MUM: Simon. What if…I mean…

SIMON: *[Gently]* Come on Mum, I'm sure she'll be fine. Let's just go.

MUM: Yes. I'll gather a few bits together…Oh God, I just keep thinking about, well, before she left to go out….

Family freezes. All exit except Mum and Dad

Scene 4

Gretel enters, dressed up.

GRETEL: I'm off.

MUM: Right love. Oh, you look nice. What time will you be back?

GRETEL: *[Offhand]* How should I know?

DAD: *[Looks up]* Don't you dare use that tone of voice in this house! And what the hell's that on your face? *[Gets up and inspects her]* Good God Margaret, she's not going out like that!

GRETEL: *[Mumbles]* It's only make-up, Dad.

DAD: Make-up? More like slap-up. You'll wash all that muck off before you go anywhere looking like a...

GRETEL: *[Defiant]* Mum likes it. She says I look nice.

DAD: Oh does she? Margaret?

MUM: Well I...

DAD: So I'm not even supported in my own house?

MUM: It's...oh. Well, it's...not that bad... *[Tails off]*

DAD: I don't believe this! You're ganging up on me, the pair of you. Your daughter is looking like I don't know what and you're just...

MUM: Well, um, maybe it is...a bit overdone...don't you think Gretel? *[Pleading to Gretel]* Maybe just tone it down a little, you know?

DAD: *[Satisfied]* Listen to your Mum now. She knows best.

[Goes back to watching TV]

GRETEL: You are such a hypocrite. I don't believe it. I thought you were on my side.

DAD: Enough! One more word and I'll…

GRETEL: What? Oh sure. Hammer me! Like your precious bits of wood? Huh? Well, I'm off while you two carry on playing Happy Families. Thanks Mum! *[Exits, slamming door]*

DAD: I am not putting up with that in this house, I tell you Margaret.

MUM: Yes Walter.

DAD: No way! God knows how she ended up like that. She's a misfit that girl is. Disgraceful. Anyway, hope you've got something nice on the go for me tonight.

MUM: Oh, oh yes. Your favourite, Walter. Liver and onions.

DAD: That's more like it. Now what's on next? *[Points remote at TV]*

Blackout. Mum and Dad exit

Scene 5

HAZEL: *[Offstage]* Come on then, we'll go upstairs.

Enter Gretel and friends. Rowan dumps an armful of clothes on floor

Let's clear a bit of space here. *[Moves furniture from scene 4]* Give us a hand Cindy, and you Olly, no sitting down!

CINDY: Yeah, sure. Where do you want it? [*Removes her jacket*]

OLLY: [*Reluctantly*] But I'm saving my energy for later!

ROWAN: [*Picks up dress*] Hey, haven't seen this one. Is it new?

HAZEL: Mmmm. [*Still moving things*]

ROWAN: Not bad.

HAZEL: What? Oh, yes. Birthday present. Do you really think it's OK? Now then, this pile here needs serious attention. You lot can be my stylists. We all know I'm prone to an occasional fashion disaster. Just remember, I trust you, so don't let me walk out of here looking like the beast of the bag lady!

SAM: What *is* this? [*Holds up top*]

HAZEL: Er. Mum gave it to me. You don't like it?

SAM: Are you kidding?

ROWAN: OK, let's start a reject pile.

GRETEL: Better put me on it then.

OLLY: [*Laughing*] What do you mean?

GRETEL: Oh, nothing. Just not really feeling in a party mood, that's all.

ROWAN: So, bye-bye sad top. [*Drops it*] Let's find something to keep you company. [*Rummages*] Aaaargh! You are NOT ever allowed to wear this! It's gone. In fact, where's the bin?

HAZEL: [*Laughs*] It's not that bad is it? Okay. It is!

CINDY: What about this? I bet it looks nice on.

GRETEL: Ha, you've got no taste either. [*Cindy looks hurt*] Joke!

SAM: Come on, let's get organised here, we haven't got long. We need to weed out the absolute no-nos first.

GRETEL: Here's one. [Holds up Cindy's jacket, drops it on reject pile]

CINDY: Er, that's mine.

GRETEL: Is it? Ah well, good job it's dark out, eh?

Cindy looks down

Oh for goodness sake, I don't mean it. You can stop doing the hurt puppy look! [Sits down]

HAZEL: What about this? [Holds up item, all shake heads] This? [Holds another]

ROWAN: Put it on the maybe pile. [Picks something] Now I do like this.

Sam, Rowan and Cindy continue helping Hazel to choose in the background, murmuring quiet, improvised responses to clothes as they help Hazel get ready

GRETEL: [Sighs] I'm bored.

OLLY: [Sits next to Gretel] So, how come no party mood then, eh?

GRETEL: What? Oh, you know.

OLLY: No, I don't. What?

GRETEL: It's …nothing.

OLLY: Doesn't look like it. Come on.

GRETEL: [Sighs] It's John.

OLLY: And?

GRETEL: Oh, Olly… I don't know what's going on. Something's changed, it's not like it was. To be honest, I'm sure he fancies someone else.

OLLY: Really? Who?

GRETEL: Just someone. I've got a few ideas.

OLLY: What are you going to do then?

GRETEL: I don't know. What do you think?

OLLY: You still like him, don't you? *[Gretel nods]* You don't want to finish with him?

GRETEL: I'm just wondering if he's about to dump me. I simply want things to be like they used to.

OLLY: So, talk to him.

GRETEL: Yeah, I suppose you're right. It's just, I can't think what to say. I could launch into 'I really want to make this work' and he might be on the verge of the big heave-ho.

OLLY: Well, you won't know 'til you try, will you? He is going tonight, isn't he?

GRETEL: Yeah, I said I'd see him there.

OLLY: Well, there you are then. First step.

ROWAN: *[Shouts]* That's the one! Won't object to being seen with you in that, will we?

CINDY: Perfect!

SAM: Great, let's get going then. Finishing touches everyone! On a count of ten! *[Sam shouts out the numbers from ten to one]*

On each number, group adopts a different freeze- frame tableau of getting ready e.g. applying make-up, doing hair. On one, they are ready

And move it!

All hold exit tableau. During blackout, change tableau position to 'arrival'. Partygoers, Maddy's gang and Chris enter

Scene 6

Partygoers, Maddy's gang and Chris (the host) in different freeze-frame party tableaux as lights come up. Friends' group mime knocking on door.

CHRIS: *[Unfreezes]* Hi! Come in, come in! *[As s/he opens mimed door, party music blares and partygoers come to life]* Stick any coats in the hall. *[Shouting]* There's food and stuff in the kitchen if you want.

OLLY: Great, loads of people here already.

HAZEL: Looks promising.

CHRIS: Have fun. Catch you later.

SAM: I'm thirsty.

CINDY: Me too.

SAM: Come on then. Anyone else? Rowan?

ROWAN: Yeah, yeah. Just looking to see who's here. Hey, who's he?

Hazel, Sam, Cindy and Rowan weave their way to the back. Music volume lowers

GRETEL: Can you see him anywhere?

OLLY: Um...no. D'you want me to help you look?

GRETEL: Don't worry. I'd better do this by myself. I'll come and find you if he's not here.

OLLY: Okay. Good luck. Hope it's not as bad as you think.

Gretel exits. Olly joins Rowan and others returning with plastic cups. Chris approaches

CHRIS: Okay then? Got drinks sorted?

ROWAN: Bet you're glad your parents aren't around. Did they know you'd invite this many?

CHRIS: Ah...I just kind of mentioned how I 'might' invite a couple of friends round to keep me company!

SAM: *[Laughs]* Better say your prayers then. You're so dead!

CHRIS: No way! They won't find out. They'll never know.

ROWAN: Right! Dream on. What about the neighbours? The mess?

CHRIS: Oh...my...God! Ah well, all the more reason to *[melodramatic]* 'Eat, drink and be merry. For tomorrow we die!' Or whatever. Come on, you've missed half the fun already.

HAZEL: Like what?

SAM: Yeah, fill us in!

CHRIS: Well, let's see, you missed...this:

Clicks fingers, all partygoers freeze. Friends' group watch. Music changes abruptly to indicate a flashback. Groups of partygoers improvise/mime various scenes. Those not involved in each scene stay in frozen tableaux. CHRIS REPEATS: And this, *and* Not forgetting...*to start each new scenario and clicks fingers to start and stop scenes. Chris can also stop a scene in the middle to get friends to speculate on what happened next, then restart it to find out. Music changes for each scene*

CHRIS: So you see, it's all happening here!

ROWAN: I'll say! Don't want to miss anything else do we? Come on, let's find some action of our own.

Friends exit, dancing. John enters among other partygoers

GRETEL: *[Enters]* John! John! There you are. I've been looking all over.

JOHN: Ah, Gretel.

GRETEL: Don't I get a hug or anything?

JOHN: Shall we go somewhere a bit...quieter?

GRETEL: OK. That sounds nicer. *[Moves to front of stage. Music volume lowers, party continues silently in background]* So, where were we? *[Moves to put arms around him. John steps back]*

JOHN: Gretel, I...

GRETEL: What's the matter?

JOHN: I think we need to talk, don't we?

GRETEL: *[Resigned]* Yeah. All right. I know, I was going to say the same. Do you want to start or shall I?

JOHN: I will. I...um...I want you to know that I still want us to be friends...

GRETEL: *[Butts in]* Are you finishing with me?

JOHN: Well, I...

GRETEL: Because you fancy someone else! I knew it!

JOHN: No!

GRETEL: Oh, come off it, do I look stupid?

JOHN: I don't know what you're talking about. It's nothing to do with anyone else...

GRETEL: Yeah! And I live in a gingerbread house!

JOHN: I'm telling you, I promise...

GRETEL: Don't waste your breath, I even know who it is.

JOHN: For God's sake Gretel, there's nothing to know. This is about us...about you.

GRETEL: What are you talking about?

JOHN: You. You've...changed. You're, I don't know, different.

GRETEL: What do you mean? No I'm not! Look at me: same old Gretel.

JOHN: It's what's underneath.

GRETEL: You're just trying to make excuses.

JOHN: No...oh, what's the use? Forget it. I'm going outside. [He moves off, exasperated]

GRETEL: But we haven't finished talking yet. You can't do this to me. Please. Wait! [Gretel runs out after him]

As they exit, they almost collide with Maddy and gang entering

HOLLY: Ah look, it must be bin day. I see the rubbish is going out!

IVY: Nice one, Holly!

MADDY: I can't imagine what she sees in him. About time they split up.

IVY: Absolutely. Hey, listen, I've got a good one: what do you get when you cross a tart with a nerd? [Pause] A turd!

All laugh nastily

JO: Wish I had your way with words Ivy. You are pure poison!

IVY: [Smug] I do my best. Practise, practise, practise those perfect put-downs!

MADDY: Well, not a lot happening here. [Spots someone walking past] Oh - my - God! What does she think she looks like? [Loudly] It wasn't supposed to be fancy dress, y'know! [Laughs. Slight pause, looks at gang, they laugh forcedly. Maddy looks back at Jo] Mind you, looks as though you both shop in the same place. *[Others laugh, Jo sulks]*

JO: *[To Lorraine]* Well, I don't know why you're laughing, Lorraine. You've been wearing that top since last year. Can't you afford anything else?

IVY AND HOLLY: Ooooh miaiowwww!

Enter Cindy

MADDY: All right Jo, save it. I spy…a mouse in the house. Tell me, shall we…?

They slowly form a semi-circle around Cindy who looks alarmed

Ah, look girls, it's frightened. The 'ikkle mousie's looking scared.

IVY: Well, I hope it doesn't wet itself. They do, you know. Mice are incontinent.

HOLLY: What does that mean?

MADDY: *[Ignores Holly]* Nice mousie, we only want to play. *[Pause]* Or *is* it a mouse?

LORRAINE: Don't know Maddy. Looks more like a gerbil to me.

JO: Or a hamster - look at those teeth! *[Laughs]*

MADDY: I was thinking more like a rat. The sort that lives in a sewer…

IVY: And carries diseases.

MADDY: Ah, but it can't be. Rats breed all the time. And let's face it. Nothing would fancy that!

LORRAINE: Maybe her family couldn't afford a dog. They had her instead.

Enter Olly and Rowan

OLLY: Look.

ROWAN: Cindy!

Cindy dashes to them. Rowan, Olly and Cindy exit

MADDY: Ah, see how it runs! See ya Cindy, enjoyed our chat.

JO: Pity they turned up.

HOLLY: Swots. Top set suckers.

IVY: Bet they know what incontinent means though.

MADDY: Sure, but only 'cos they are! [*Sings Three Blind Mice up to 'see how they run'*]

Silence

IVY: So, what's next, Maddy?

MADDY: Dunno. I'm bored. Let's see if we can find some real fun. Come on.

Gang exits. Partygoers move forward

PARTYGOER 1: There she goes, the Gorgon Medusa.

PARTYGOER 2: The Gordon what? What are you on about?

PARTYGOER 1: This is just too funny. What did you think 'Maddy' was short for? Her real name: it's Medusa.

PARTYGOER 3: And? Why's that hilarious?

PARTYGOER 1: Because it suits her so well. Don't you know who Medusa was?

PARTYGOERS 2 & 3: No.

PARTYGOER1: Well, that's kind of why it's funny: neither did her mum when she chose the name. She just thought it sounded classy.

PARTYGOER 3: Go on.

Sam drifts over to join group

PARTYGOER 1: Well, according to someone I met, her mum was

working in a pet shop while she was pregnant and the resident python was called Medusa.

PARTYGOER 4: Oh...! [*Gets it*] You mean, she's named after a snake. How fitting!

PARTYGOER 1: Yeah, but it gets even better. Medusa was a woman in a Greek myth, well, not even a woman - one of three monsters called gorgons who were so terrible that anyone who looked at them turned to stone. Medusa was the worst because she had hair made of snakes.

PARTYGOER 4: I am so enjoying this! No wonder she's got a forked tongue.

PARTYGOER 1: Anyway, ever since she found out what it really means, Maddy won't let *anyone* call her Medusa, even her mum. She goes mad. Who can blame her, named after a snake-haired monster!

SAM: Perfect!

PARTYGOER 3: We can't possibly keep this to ourselves.

PARTYGOER 2: This requires some serious stirring!

This group exits. Partygoers 5 and 6 join Sam

PARTYGOER 5: What was that about?

PARTYGOER 6: Something about Maddy?

SAM: Oh yes! Come with me while I get a drink. I'll tell all.

Exit. Enter Maddy and gang

LORRAINE: Maybe we should go and dance or something.

MADDY: Are you kidding, I don't 'do' dancing.

JO: Well, we will. You can watch. [*Sees Maddy's look*] Okay, maybe not.

Enter partygoers 5 and 6

PARTYGOER 6: Hey! Medusa!

MADDY: You what? What did you call me?

PARTYGOER 5: Medusssssssssa! It is your name, issssn't it?

IVY: What are they going on about?

MADDY: And who the hell told you that?

PARTYGOER 6: So it's true!

PARTYGOER 5: Nicccccce name!

MADDY: I said, who told you?

PARTYGOER 6: Does it matter?...One of those girls who hang
    round with Rowan. [*To partygoer 5*] What's her
    name? Is it...Gretel?

MADDY: Right!

HOLLY: Wait for us!

MADDY: No, I'll deal with this by myself. [*Exits furiously*]

Gang look at each other then exit in opposite direction

PARTYGOER 5: No - Sam I think. Isn't it?

PARTYGOER 6: Dunno. Whatever. Well [*Ironic*] that cleared the
    air a bit.

PARTYGOER 5: Weren't you scared?

PARTYGOER 6: Course not. She's all mouth that one. [*Thinks*]
    Well, maybe a little, but it was worth it. Come on.

Exit. Blackout

Scene 7

Gretel in hospital robe, clothed underneath. All cast with backs to audience, physically forming tree shapes around her to represent forest. Gretel wanders warily among them - tree shapes shift and move, making her passage difficult. Cast echo some of her words to create eerie whisper.

GRETEL: I don't like it here. It's dark and there are eyes among the leaves. I lost the path ages ago. Now everywhere looks the same - trees tripping and tricking, scratching. [*Shouts*] Stop watching me! Stop whispering behind my back! I know you're there. You're always there. Come on then, show your faces.

Whispering echoes continue. Slowly, Maddy and gang emerge, whispering and repeating to each other as they advance

'Nibble, nibble little mouse, who's that nibbling at our house?'

GRETEL: Oh, not you. I didn't mean you. Why don't you leave me alone? Get off me. I don't want to go with you. I don't want to remember.

They close in and remove her hospital gown and spin her around

MADDY: Too late, sweetie pie.

Lights change. Artificially bright. Sound of school bell. Cast become pupils in school. Lunchtime. Improvise the chaos and snatched conversations of pupils just out of lessons. Maddy and gang watch Gretel and improvise conversations about how much they dislike Gretel's achievement in the previous lesson. Rest of cast disperse, as though to lunch

MADDY: It's Miss Perfect.

HOLLY: Thinks she's so clever.

IVY: Knows all the answers.

MADDY: Doesn't know it all though, does she?

GRETEL: [*Turns, innocent*] Sorry, what?

Silence while gang look at each other

MADDY: [*Snide*] Talking '*about*' you, not '*to*' you.

GRETEL: Oh...I...oh.[*She exits*]

Gang laughs. Brief blackout

MADDY: I'm bored.

JO: Not for much longer! I spy with my little eye something beginning with 'c'...

Gretel and Olly enter

HOLLY: Creeps? Cows? Cringe-worthy cows?

They trip Gretel up

LORRAINE: Oopsy Daisy.

MADDY: Better watch where you're going.

IVY: You could have hurt someone.

OLLY: [*Helps Gretel up*] You did that on purpose.

MADDY: [*Intimidating*] You want to say that again, a bit louder?

GRETEL: It's all right. Come on.

Exit Gretel and Olly

MADDY: [*Calls after*] Your bus is leaving soon. Make sure you're under it.

JO: Kiddies.

HOLLY: What?

JO: Beginning with 'c'.

IVY: That's 'k', stupid! As in kicking 'k', not curly!

Brief blackout. Lights up. Gang have a schoolbag

HOLLY: Look what I 'found'.

IVY: Whose is it?

MADDY: Give it here. *[Empties it]* Aha *[Holds file or exercise book. Reads]* 'Gretel 'Annoying' Ashwell! English Language.' Ooh look...and she's done her homework already.

IVY: *[Has been looking in pencil case, holds up glue stick and scissors]* Shall we add a little something to it?

MADDY: Excellent!

IVY: I'll get 'stuck in' then. *[Glues pages together]* Here! Now she really is 'stuck up'. *[Hands scissors to Lorraine]* Do something useful.

JO: Here you go, geography assignment. *[Hands sheet of paper to Lorraine who folds it and cuts it into a doily]*

LORRAINE: What do you think? Pretty, isn't it?

HOLLY: Quick, here she comes!

They shove everything back in messily, drop bag and exit. Gretel enters with Cindy, Olly, and Sam

GRETEL: Oh, there it is. *[Picks it up]* Hey, wait a minute. *[Pulls out 'doily']* Oh God! Now I'll have to do it again.

SAM: No way. You should report it.

GRETEL: Oh yeah, and make even more trouble for myself? I don't think so.

Blackout. Exit Olly and Sam. Enter Cindy

GRETEL: *[Sounding offhand]* You got your coursework finished then?

CINDY: Finally! Actually, John gave me some help with it when we were in the library. You're really lucky, Gretel. He's very...patient.

GRETEL: Maybe that depends...on who he's with.

Enter Maddy and gang

MADDY: It's the gruesome twosome!

JO: Geeks.

HOLLY: Freaks.

IVY: Geek freaks! That's it. New name! Where are the rest of them?

MADDY: Like I care.

GRETEL: Don't look over, just walk. [*They move past*]

MADDY: Oh my God, have you *seen* what she's got on? [*Talking about Cindy's trainers or socks or jacket*]

Cindy hesitates, looks back

That's right, you! Where did you get the [trainers/socks/jacket] from? A charity shop?

IVY: More like a jumble sale!

GRETEL: I think you'll find it was the dustbin actually!

CINDY: What?

MADDY: Whoa! Nice one! [*Looks questioningly at Gretel*] Careful...

Gretel and Cindy turn and move almost off stage

CINDY: I...I don't get it.

GRETEL: [*Hisses*] Joke! I *told* you not to look back, stupid!

Gang exit. Cindy exits. Blackout. Gretel alone on stage mimes hand washing

MADDY: [Offstage] Quick! Into the loos! Right, who's got them?

Gang enter. Gretel looks up, silence

GRETEL: [Nervously] All right?

MADDY: It speaks!

LORRAINE: It squeaks!

IVY: Where's your little friend?

GRETEL: We're not joined at the hip. And just because she hangs around doesn't make her a friend either.

MADDY: Oooh. Sharp too. Mind you don't cut yourself. [Turns away] Come on Jo, I know you've got some. Hand them over.

Jo reluctantly brings cigarette packet from pocket. Maddy snatches it

Thank you. Now, where's the lighter? [Turns, sees Gretel] You still here? Want a picture? [Poses]

GRETEL: No...um...sorry.

HOLLY: Maybe she wants one too.

LORRAINE: Her! She's never sniffed anyone else's fag smoke, never mind inhaled - have you? [She looms over Gretel]

GRETEL: [Bluffs] Actually I have. I mean...I do.

LORRAINE: [Mimicking] Oh 'actually, yes. Actually, I've been smoking since I was four, actually.' Not.

Silence, Gretel turns to go

MADDY: Interesting. Prove it.

GRETEL: [Nervous] Sure. But...I don't have any with me.

IVY: What a surprise. Go on, creep back to your freaky friends.

MADDY: Wait. [*Holds out packet to Gretel. Pause*] Let's see what she's made of.

JO: [*Through clenched teeth*] I haven't got that many, Maddy.

GRETEL: [*Pause. Then, slowly*] All right.

She reaches out. Blackout. Sound of extended, violent coughing covers exit of gang and Gretel and entrance of family

Scene 8

At hospital. Family seated in a line thus: George, Dad, Mum, Simon.

.

DAD: [*Coughs loudly*] These damn places are enough to make anyone ill. What the hell's keeping them? Anyone would think they'd gone on holiday.

MUM: They said it shouldn't be long, just a few more tests and then we can see her again.

DAD: Well, I'm not hanging around all day. We were here half the night. [*He fidgets uncomfortably*]

GEORGE: All right Dad, I know we're all worried.

DAD: Hmmmm.

[*Tense silence*]

MUM: She looks so helpless, wired up to all those things, so…lost, my lost little girl.

SIMON: She'll be OK Mum, you'll see.

DAD: Huh, now we're a brain surgeon are we? What do

you know?

MUM: *[Looks pleadingly at Dad]* Walter…

Dad rolls his eyes and sighs. Silence

GEORGE: We should have stopped to get some flowers or something.

DAD: Flowers! What on earth for? She wouldn't see 'em, state she's in! Anyway we've got our own little flower here. *[Shrugs towards Simon]*

SIMON: Honestly Dad, I don't believe you. That's Gretel, your only daughter in there. Do you even care? I haven't heard you say one thing to show you've got the slightest human feeling. You're like a…a block of wood - a block of your precious wood.

MUM: Simon, please! Your Dad, well, he's…he's…

DAD: He's what? Yes, do please tell me what I am. *[Pause, to Simon]* So, the worm turns.

SIMON: This isn't about me! It's about Gretel.

DAD: Yes, and I'm sure we all want to know what the hell Gretel was up to get herself into a mess like this.

SIMON: This is unbelievable. You wouldn't know a feeling if it sawed you in half. I can't stand this, I'm going to get a coffee or something. I'll be back later, Mum, OK?

Simon exits

DAD: How dare he? Well he needn't think he can get away with it either. Oh no! Honestly, what with his fancy footwork and her getting her head filled up with grand ideas by those teachers of hers…*[Turns on Mum]* And as for you! Always too soft on them…No wonder we've got these problems now. Authority! That's what they need. Never harmed me.

GEORGE: *[Quietly]* Why don't you pick on someone your own size for a change, Dad?

DAD: What?...George?

GEORGE: Like me. *[Silence. Stares at Dad]*

DAD: *[Looks down, confused]* But son...

GEORGE: You know what Dad? We work hard, you and I, we have a good laugh down the pub. So why do you have to keep on doing it? Picking on your own kids; having a go at Mum all the time? I'm sick of it.

DAD: Now wait a minute, boy, I'll...

GEORGE: No. I'm not your 'boy' any more. *You* wait. Simon was right. We *[indicates himself and Mum]* are here for Gretel. So why don't you go and take out your nasty temper on a nice little plank somewhere else instead?

DAD: But George. I can't just let them get away with...I thought you...

GEORGE: So think again, Dad. Time to go. Gretel needs her mum now.

DAD: Well, well, I never in my life, I...I've got things to do. Can't stop work for every little accident. Waste of good time this is. Need to...to get on back at the yard. *[Backs off, exits]*

MUM: *[Softly]* You go. Leave me alone. Leave her alone.

GEORGE: Sorry Mum. I should have said something earlier... it's just not on...I'll go and check up on Simon and get that coffee.

MUM: *[Hugging George]* Thanks Georgie.

He exits. Pause

Someone throw her a white pebble or a little crumb of comfort. But not him. Never him. It's so hard. Help her find the way. Oh Gretel, please wake up, please.

Enter Olly, Rowan and Hazel

OLLY: Mrs Ashwell.

MUM: Oh.

OLLY: Sorry, didn't mean to startle you.

ROWAN: We wanted to know about Gretel. There wasn't any answer at your house, so we got the bus here.

MUM: Yes, of course. That's very kind of you, very thoughtful. You're good girls. Did you take the day off school?

Friends look at each other

HAZEL: It's Sunday, Mrs Ashwell.

MUM: Of course it is. Sorry. It just seems so long since last night, like weeks have passed since then…and yet it's less than twelve hours.

ROWAN: So, how is she? It sounded really serious from what the police said.

MUM: Well, she hasn't regained consciousness at all. They've said she's in a coma.

OLLY: That's what we heard.

HAZEL: But she is going to be all right, isn't she?

MUM: Oh, Hazel…I…The doctor said he'd come and explain what's going on as soon as they've finished this latest test. He said they wouldn't be long, though that was a while ago. *[Tails off]* If only I knew what happened. You were with her. Surely you know something?

HAZEL: We've been over and over it. We all arrived at the party together but then Gretel went off.

OLLY: To find John.

MUM: Of course, John. Where's he? What does he say?

OLLY: I just kept getting the answer service when I tried ringing his house this morning and I think his mobile must be switched off.

HAZEL: And we couldn't find him last night, after... afterwards.

ROWAN: We know Gretel found him though. Sam saw them talking early on, but that's all. [Pause] Sam sends her love by the way. She works on a Sunday - couldn't get out of it.

HAZEL: Oh, and Cindy's mum said she's feeling really off-colour today. But, well, we couldn't just wait around at home all day. I hope you don't mind us coming.

MUM: Of course not. It's nice to know she's got such caring friends. Besides, I need you to tell me everything, any little thing about last night that might help. Who was the last to see her?

OLLY: Me. Like I said, we arrived and she disappeared to find John and then none of us saw her again for ages, not until...

ROWAN: The music went off and everyone was crowding outside and shouting and running and pushing and getting hysterical.

MUM: So, if you didn't find her, who did?

ROWAN: Chris, you know, whose party it was.

HAZEL: And then there were a couple of Year 11 girls we don't really know. One of them had done a first aid course so she sort of took charge.

OLLY: And the other one rang for an ambulance. Chris was useless. He just stood there in a daze, saying 'What am I going to tell my parents?'

MUM: But surely *someone* must know or must have seen… I don't know. I mean, it sounds like half your school was there. Didn't Chris say if there was anyone else outside?

HAZEL: No, he just said Gretel was by herself, lying on the patio. No one else was there, or at least not when Chris went out.

OLLY: You're right though. Someone definitely knows and isn't saying.

ROWAN: But we've got a pretty good idea who. We've talked about nothing else since last night and it all adds up.

MUM: What does? Tell me!

ROWAN: Has Gretel ever mentioned Maddy?

MUM: Maddy? [*Thinks*] I don't think so. Not that I remember. Why? Who is she?

ROWAN: She's bad news, that's who she is - and the sacks of venom she calls mates. They've been giving Gretel a hard time.

Hazel: Not *just* Gretel, all of us. They can't bear anyone who does well or who works in lessons.

OLLY: They've got names for us, call us things behind our backs, talk about us like we're not there, that kind of thing. But recently, it's got much worse.

ROWAN: Cindy's totally freaked out by them. They were vicious to her last night and she's been so quiet the past few weeks, I think it's really getting to her.

MUM: But Gretel's never said anything.

OLLY:	No, I don't suppose she has. We couldn't even persuade her to tell the teachers - she reckoned it would just cause more trouble.
MUM:	So you think this girl, Maddy? And her friends have something to do with what happened. Are you sure?
ROWAN:	Well, we can't prove it.
OLLY:	Yet.

Enter Doctor

DOCTOR:	Mrs Ashwell, I'm ready to see you now. Is your husband here?
MUM:	Oh...he...had to go.
DOCTOR:	OK, then. If you'd like to come with me?
MUM:	Of course. [*To friends*] Will you wait? I'll be back and then maybe you can see her.

Mum exits. Friends look at each other

| ROWAN: | I think we should confront Maddy tomorrow, see how she and her vipers react. |
| HAZEL: | It seems weird to think about going to school. Can you imagine what everyone's going to be saying? |

Exit

Scene 9

This scene is to be improvised. Pupils at school, grouped in gossiping tableaux. As lights come up, first group improvise speculations about what happened to Gretel at the party, while the other groups freeze. The scene as a whole should work like a sensationalized version of Chinese whispers, where each group describes in turn what they've heard or what they suppose happened. When improvising these short scenes, performers should aim for a tabloid style exaggeration and embellishment. None of them actually knows at this point what caused Gretel's coma, so they can speculate about a range of possibilities e.g. falling from a window/fight/allergic reaction/ overdose/victim/attention-seeking. The scene ends with Rowan's entrance.

ROWAN: *[Shouts]* You don't know anything. It's a skull fracture. We went to the hospital yesterday. And no, the police don't know how it happened…yet - but they'll find out. So just give your fevered imaginations a rest. This is sick.

She exits. Pupils exit, murmuring and discussing this information

Scene 10

Mum at home with a bag of apples in her hand.

MUM: I'm so tired, but I've got to, I've got to…yes, apples
for Gretel. Not that she can eat them at the
moment. Not that she can *do* anything. *[Pause]*
Wally's at work. One less thing to worry about.
Maybe he's right: it *is* all my fault. I've been too soft
all along. *[Sighs]* He was a bit shocked when she first
arrived. 'My happy accident' I called her. 'Be
different if it was a boy, complete the set,' he said.
But she was bonny and bright and he liked that.
Happy days. *[Sighs]* But then Gretel started to grow
up, you know how girls do, get minds of their own.
And the last couple of months she's got so stubborn,
moody too. And answering back, saying such things!
What could I do? But he wouldn't stand for it. Not
at all. She'd always been a good girl and suddenly, to
him, everything she did was wrong. Oh I know she
hasn't been easy, but he came down so hard every
time. And it was always 'the boys' this and then
especially 'George that' and she got left out. His
rules, his ways and none of us allowed to step outside
them. So here I am, caught in the middle. Why do I
have to take sides in my own family? And then
everything builds up and Gretel takes it out on me.
Everyone takes it out on me. *[Lifts apples out to check
them]* An apple a day, but, damn…bruised! They're
all bruised. *[Sobs. Hurls them to the floor]*

Blackout

Scene 11

Gretel and Mum two months ago. Simon enters as Gretel speaks.

GRETEL: So, will you talk to Mrs Keatley about it at parents' evening?

MUM: Of course, love.

SIMON: What's that?

GRETEL: Mrs Keatley, my history teacher - she said that my work was already way above the standard for Year 10 GCSE, and that I should definitely think about staying on into the Sixth Form and consider 'A' levels.

SIMON: Wow. Is that what you want to do?

GRETEL: Absolutely! What's more, she said that even though it's a long way off, she thought I might get a lot out of studying History at university. Can you imagine? Getting away from this dump?

MUM: Gretel!

GRETEL: I mean it.

SIMON: If only! Sounds wonderful. Good for you. You certainly work hard enough. How come you got all the brains in the family? It's not fair!

GRETEL: *[Giggling]* Yeah, well they definitely bypassed you and George!

SIMON: *[Good-naturedly]* Cheeky cow! I'm still faster than you, though. *[He rushes at her to tickle her, they shriek and laugh]*

Dad and George enter

DAD: Good God, what's all this racket? You're like a couple of babies.

They stop abruptly

GRETEL: Sorry, I was just telling Mum and Simon…

DAD: Tea ready yet?

MUM: Nearly.

GEORGE: Great! I'm starving. Smells good, Mum.

DAD: He works up a good appetite, George does. He's a hard worker, no mistake. *[He sits, unfolds newspaper]* I'll have a cup of tea while we're waiting.

GEORGE: I'll stick the kettle on.

DAD: No you won't. *[Indicates Gretel]* She will. You put your feet up.

MUM: I'll do it.

GEORGE: *[To Mum]* Have I got time to get changed?

MUM: About five minutes, I should think. *[Exit]*

GEORGE: Okay then. *[Exit]*

GRETEL: Will you be going to the parents' evening tomorrow Dad?

DAD: *[Behind the paper]* That's your mother's department.

GRETEL: But would you for this one?

DAD: Give me the creeps, schools do. Anyway, I'll be busy.

GRETEL: Doing what?

DAD: Just busy, right?

GRETEL: But my teacher wants to see you both.

DAD: Why? What sort of trouble are you in?

GRETEL: I'm not! She wants to talk about my 'academic future'.

DAD: *[Not listening]* You what?

GRETEL: About me carrying on with History, not just to 'A' level, but perhaps even to university.

DAD: *[Lowers paper, looks at her, then raises paper again]* What would you want to do that for?

GRETEL: She said I should aim high, that I've got real potential.

Silence from Dad

         She said…

DAD: *[Breaks in]* Can I not get a moment's peace at the end of the day?

GRETEL: But Dad! This is important!

DAD: *[Finally lowers paper]* Who to? Not to me it isn't. If your Mrs Whatsername is going to start filling your mind with grand ideas, perhaps she'd like to pay for them too, eh?

Enter Mum

GRETEL: But she just…

DAD: For heaven's sake girl, watch my lips. No. I mean, what damn use is History to anyone?

GRETEL: Mrs Keatley says it's only through 'understanding the past that we can change the future.'

DAD: And what's that supposed to mean? Mumbo jumbo. In fact, I've a good mind to come to this parents' evening after all, give her a piece of my mind about filling up young girls' heads with fancy thoughts.

GRETEL: You can't do that.

DAD: Don't you try and tell me what I can or can't do. I'll tell you this much. You can forget about university: waste of time, waste of *my* money. Face facts, you'll still end up with some bloke, having babies, and you don't need brains to do that - look at your mother.

GRETEL: *[Appeals]* Mum? *[Under breath]* Which century is he living in?

MUM: Maybe we should talk about this some other time.

DAD: I've said all I've got to say. *[Picks up newspaper]*

MUM: Well. Er, tea's just about ready.

GRETEL: Is that it? Once again, you're not going to say anything? Just carry on, pretend everything's normal, hope it'll just go away if you ignore it for long enough. I don't know which of you is worse.

MUM: Now, come on...love *[Reaches to touch Gretel. Gretel pulls away]* Let's just...change the subject until after tea, when we've all calmed down.

GRETEL: *[Shakes head in disbelief]* Did you hear anything I just said? Dad's right about you. You're practically brain dead. *[She turns to leave]*

MUM: Where are you going?

GRETEL: Upstairs.

MUM: What about your tea?

GRETEL: Not hungry.

MUM: I'll save you some then, shall I, for after you've finished your homework?

GRETEL: Homework? You are joking? After *that*? *[To Simon]* What are you staring at? *[Exits]*

DAD: *[Lowers his paper]*A lot of fuss about nothing. Well, don't just stand there. Give George a shout and get the food on the table.

Blackout

Scene 12

At the hospital.

DOCTOR: The brain scan has shown us that Gretel has a cerebral oedema. That's a swelling of the brain.

MUM: A swelling, what, like a bruise? So it will go down?

DOCTOR: Obviously that's what we hope. We've started her on steroids to reduce the swelling and at the moment she's on a ventilator...

MUM: *[Panics]* Oh my God! Did she stop breathing?

DOCTOR: No, no. We're using the ventilator to over-ventilate her. You see, if you reduce the carbon dioxide in the bloodstream, it helps reduce the swelling in the brain.

MUM: Oh. But what...why is she in a coma? Why won't she wake up?

DOCTOR: Well, as you know, Gretel was brought in with a small external injury to the back of her head. Now that we've had a chance to see inside, we've discovered that she has a hairline fracture and she's also suffered what's known as a 'contra coup'. This means that something has caused her brain to literally bounce and rebound inside her skull.

MUM: 'Something'? Like what?

DOCTOR: A heavy blow to the head, perhaps a fall knocking the head. It's an impact injury.

MUM: But she will recover?

DOCTOR: We're in a 'wait and see' situation right now. I wish I could be more specific, but we have to watch the swelling. On the plus side, we do know that the brain has some quite extraordinary powers of recovery. However, because it has suffered damage, Gretel's brain has shut down all non-essential functions for the time being.

MUM: So we wait, that's all?

DOCTOR: I'm afraid so.

MUM: What did you say it was called again?

DOCTOR: Contra coup - it's French - it means 'against or opposite knock'.

MUM: [Thinking] So, someone else must have been involved.

DOCTOR: It's always possible that she fell by herself, but from the position of the injury, [Pause] unlikely.

MUM: [Repeats, dazed] Contra coup…

Cast take up 'contra coup' as an eerie echo while bringing onstage screen for shadow show. Doctor and Mum exit

Scene 13

Music from party scene.

MADDY: *[Voiced from off stage]* When I get my hands on that piece of dirt, she'll wish she never heard my name!

Music becomes progressively slower/distorted. Scene to be enacted through shadow play behind screen or with masked performers to hide identity. Three performers use dumbshow to illustrate what happened at the party. Performer 1 observes, performers 2 and 3 mime physical conflict. Performer 1 exits. Scene ends when Performer 3 is pushed backwards and falls. See page 63 for further detailed suggestions. Read Scene 14 for details of exact events.

Scene 14

School bell sounds. Sam, Cindy and Hazel enter, walking from a lesson.

SAM: Rowan said to meet in five minutes.

SIMON: *[Enters and runs up to them]* There you are, what's happening?

SAM: We're on our way to the drama room. It's nice and quiet there. Thought we'd skip lunch.

SIMON: Fine, I've got no appetite at the moment anyway. What about the others? Have they found out any more yet?

HAZEL: Rowan's gone to find John's tutor to see if he
           registered today.

SIMON: You mean he still hasn't turned up yet? Where the
           hell is he?

SAM: That's what we want to know. There was no answer
           at his house all day yesterday and we couldn't find
           him at break.

*All exit. Enter Olly in drama room. Puts down her bag and begins
carrying in chairs from side. Enter Rowan and John*

ROWAN: Found him! He was right by the staffroom.

JOHN: *[In shock]* I only got here at the beginning of last
           lesson. I just can't believe it. I had no idea…

Enter the others.

SAM: John! Where did you crawl out from?

HAZEL: Yeah, where've you been? Nobody's seen you since
           Saturday night.

OLLY: Since, as it happens, you were talking to Gretel.
           Remember her? You know, your girlfriend, the one
           who's not here right now because, oh yes! She's in a
           coma.

JOHN: I know, Rowan just told me. It's terrible…

HAZEL: You mean you really didn't know?

OLLY: *[Cuts in]* Come on then. What happened? How come
           you weren't with her? More to the point, where the
           hell *were* you?

JOHN: Oh God. I don't know where to start. We split up.

SIMON: You what? Why?

JOHN: *[Sighs]* It feels awful to be talking about her now
           that…you know.

OLLY: Go on, you still need to tell us. How do we know you haven't got something to hide? You still haven't said where you were all this time.

JOHN: OK. We talked, I tried to tell her that I thought it wasn't working but she insisted it was because of someone else.

OLLY: And was it? Well?

JOHN: Of course not, but she didn't believe me. I went outside and she followed me. She was so convinced about me fancying someone else, she was nearly screaming at me by that point. She was out of control, unreasonable.

SIMON: And? Then what?

JOHN: I left.

ROWAN: Just like that?

JOHN: There didn't seem much point trying to say anything else. She wasn't listening. I thought it would be better if she had some time to cool down a bit. So, I found Adam and we left.

ROWAN: Adam?

JOHN: Yeah, I stayed at his place all weekend. Mum's away looking after my Gran, so that's where I've been. I also managed to leave my mobile at home in my other jeans. Then this morning I had to go to the dentist. That's why I didn't get here till after break... I really had no idea, honestly. How is she?

OLLY: Like you care.

JOHN: That's not fair.

OLLY: Oh no? I've been worried about Gretel for weeks. I knew something was going on with her because she was acting really funny in school, like she'd lost interest -

SIMON: [*Butts in*] Yeah. She's been like that at home too and stroppy with it. Couldn't be bothered working.

OLLY: [*To John*] And it was because of you, you heartless...scum. And then you leave her all by herself just when she's most upset. Great!

SAM: Yeah, you're a slimebag.

JOHN: Oh, come on. It wasn't all my fault, you know. Things had just got, well, uncomfortable between us. It was like she changed suddenly. She started getting really moody with me. I couldn't seem to do anything right and she was so sarcastic too, putting me down, making me feel about this big. [*Indicates 5cm*] To be honest, I thought she was the one who wanted to finish it.

HAZEL: OK, whatever, but that means you were still the last person to see her before...'it'.

OLLY: [*Mutters*] If he's telling the truth.

JOHN: [*Ignores Olly*] Yeah, I guess I was. She was still outside when I left her.

HAZEL: And she was still there when they found her too.

SAM: Poor Gretel.

OLLY: I keep picturing her in that hospital bed, with her arms straightened out, smooth covers, still hands, silent, not moving...[*She shudders. Silence*]

HAZEL: So, in between you leaving and Chris going outside, someone else went out there. Three guesses anyone?

ROWAN: Queen Cobra and the rest of the coven. We all know what they've done in the past. But this was their step

too far and there is no way they're going to get away
with it.

SIMON: All we need to do now is prove it.

ROWAN: Too right. I don't reckon Maddy's quite as hard as
she thinks. If we could separate her from the pack,
and

*Maddy enters as Rowan continues. Others see her just before
Rowan does*

confront her, I don't see how she could deny it. All
bullies are cowards at heart. What? *[Looks up]* Wow!
Timing!

MADDY: What are you lot gawping at? Seen my mates? No?
Right. *[Turns to go]*

ROWAN: *[Blocks her path]* I don't think so. No time like the
present.

MADDY: Oh yeah? What for?

Olly joins Rowan

ROWAN: To talk about grievous bodily harm, attempted
murder?

MADDY: That's a bit over dramatic isn't it? Save it for your
next lesson in here.

OLLY: Accurate though. We've all witnessed your little
games. We know you were out there.

MADDY: *[Slowly looks around]* OK. I admit it.

OLLY: You do?

MADDY: Yeah, I admit I was outside because I was, but I
wasn't the only one, and when I left she was still
upright, OK?

HAZEL: Yeah and my mum's the Sugar Plum Fairy!

MADDY: You can believe what you want, but if you really want to know, why don't you talk to the very last person who saw her?

ROWAN: We are. You.

MADDY: No. She knows who she is. *[Silence]* Doesn't she?

Silence. Maddy turns and slowly looks at each of the girls in turn. They all shuffle uncomfortably as the suspense becomes unbearable. Maddy's gaze finally rests on Cindy

CINDY: *[Softly]* Yes.

JOHN: What?

MADDY: See? I'll be off then.

ROWAN: You're not going anywhere. *[To Cindy]* Did she *[Indicates Maddy]* put you up to this? What did she threaten you with?

CINDY: No, it wasn't her making any threats. At least, not this time.

SAM: *[Puts arm around Cindy]* Go on.

CINDY: *[Shudders]* I wanted to say something before, wanted to tell you, but I didn't think you'd believe me and it's been going on for a while.

SAM: What has?

CINDY: It was Gretel.

ROWAN: Yes?

CINDY: She was the one.

OLLY: Who's in hospital, yes?

CINDY: No, I mean yes. I mean, she was the one making the threats.

OLLY: What are you talking about?

CINDY: Oh...I can't...Gretel, Saturday night. No one attacked her. [*Pause*] She attacked me.

Silence

SIMON: No...Gretel?

CINDY: I knew you wouldn't believe me.

SAM: It's all right. Just tell us.

CINDY: This is so awful. I don't know where to begin. There's so much you don't know. What will happen to me?

[*Draws breath*] OK. Yes, Gretel. John's not the only one she's been funny with recently. It's like she just...turned on me, only never in front of any of you. She saved it for moments when we were alone or when she [*Indicates Maddy*] was around. I don't know, but I think for some reason, Gretel maybe wanted to impress Maddy. She was certainly acting like her. I even walked in on her smoking with them once.

Disbelief from others

So, anyway, at the party, after Maddy and her lot had already had a go at me, I didn't exactly want to run into them again. I came out of the loo and saw them heading towards the living room, so I took a detour outside. I was thinking about going home and then suddenly Maddy and Gretel were in front of me, arguing. Maddy was really angry with her, something about names, and Gretel was denying it, saying she had no idea. They both turned and saw me and that's when it started. Gretel just switched immediately, started accusing me of fancying John, said I was to blame for splitting them up. Complete nonsense - he just helped me with some coursework once. But she wouldn't listen. She began pushing me, pulling my hair and stuff. Only I wouldn't do anything back. She was screaming at me, not just about John, about all sorts of things. Then I think Maddy left, saying that she was bored, and something about wet blankets flapping together, and Gretel shrieked back that she was nothing like me, she hated me. I tried to move, but she came towards me really fast, and I put my arms up in defence and I tried to just push her off and she…must have lost her balance, fallen back. The moment she was off me, I just ran for it, back to the bathroom. I really didn't know. I was afraid she'd come after me again so I stayed in there for ages, and when I came out and everyone was outside, I froze up. I couldn't say anything. It was too late. It was all too late.

Silence. Everyone, apart from Gretel, rushes on stage, improvising comments at the same time to make babble, in character, reacting to the news of what really happened. Above this hubbub, we hear Gretel shouting off stage

GRETEL: Steal my boyfriend! Miss Innocent? Not. I'll show you.

CINDY: Leave me alone. Please. Get off me. Get off. No!

All stamp simultaneously BANG All freeze. Maddy and Simon step forward

MADDY: So much fuss for the sake of a name.

SIMON: Where does it start? Who's to blame?

MADDY: At home are fists. Now I hit out.

SIMON: Dad fells his kids with scorn and doubt.

MADDY: It may look like I have all the fun

SIMON: The game is over. No one's won.

MADDY: But underneath this wooden stare

SIMON: feelings riot. Dreams dare.

MADDY: There was a girl who was betrayed.

SIMON: The perfect family? Got it made?
           Try opening the hand-carved box.

MADDY: Inside lie snakes, not curly locks.

SIMON: Love is scorned, replaced with hissing.

MADDY: Words that have their meaning missing.

SIMON: What would have happened, if she hadn't resisted?

MADDY: Does it matter? The game is twisted.

END

Rehearsal and Workshop ideas

In the beginning

The idea for *Twisted* grew out of a drama exercise conducted with a youth drama group. Try it before reading the play for the first time.

Divide into groups of four. Each group is either a group of friends, family or enemies. The object of the improvisation is for each group to react to the same piece of news - a girl is in a coma. No one knows why. Focus on the different reactions of each group to first hearing the news. When showing, start and stop each group by freezing and unfreezing them. Cut between each group to contrast snippets of response.

This exercise formed the structure for scene 3 where the action cuts between each group.

Discussion

1. Discuss why you think Gretel begins to want to impress Maddy.

2. Apart from suspecting that John likes Cindy, what other motives does Gretel have for turning on Cindy? Why does Gretel become a bully? (Look at Gretel's family life and at what happens to her self-worth. Look at how Maddy's gang treats Cindy. Finally, consider how Gretel reacts when she feels disempowered by her Dad.)

3. At the end, Simon asks, 'Where does it start? Who's to blame?' Who do you think caused this situation?

4. Dad, Gretel and Maddy all reflect something of the title. What? How?

Improvisation

1. In pairs, improvise the scene outside the party between Gretel and Cindy, which Cindy describes at the end, in her monologue. Or, in groups of three, improvise the scene between Maddy and Gretel, then Gretel and Cindy, beginning when Maddy finds Gretel in the garden. It would be possible to incorporate this improvised scene into a performance of the play as a flashback during Cindy's last monologue. It needs to be short and should aim to show Gretel at her worst. It should fully reveal Gretel as a bully herself as well as her desperation.

2. Improvise the scene between Mum and Dad when they find out what actually happened to Gretel. Think carefully about how each character may respond to the news that it was Gretel herself who launched an unprovoked attack on Cindy. Improvise the same scene between Mum, Dad and either/both Simon and George. How does the addition of Simon in this scene change it?

3. Improvise the scene between Rowan, Hazel, Sam and Olly later that day, after Cindy's revelation. How do they respond? What questions do they ask? Do they come to any conclusions? How do they now view Gretel?

4. At the end of the play it seems as though Maddy and her gang remain unchallenged about their actions. Does this trouble you? Improvise a later scene in which Maddy and gang have to face the consequences of their bullying

behaviour. Think about who could challenge them. Will it be parents, teachers, police or other characters from the play? What could anyone do or say that might genuinely make them recognize and feel the destructive impact of their taunting? Is it possible to put them in a position whereby they might voluntarily change their behaviour?

This is part of a much wider question - what are the most effective ways of confronting bullying behaviour? Should people who bully be punished, excluded, reasoned with, shocked, understood, be made to apologize/make amends or be encouraged to change their behaviour? What is likely to have the most long-term impact?

Try improvising three different scenes in which Maddy and her gang are dealt with in three different ways. Show them. Discuss firstly which versions are most dramatically satisfying and why. (Do you find the ones featuring punishment or retribution to be popular? Why?) Secondly, discuss which ones you think might actually make any of the characters reflect on their own behaviour enough to make them choose to not do it again. Why?

5. Unanswered questions. When does a play finish? Twisted deliberately ends without finding out what happens to Gretel. Why do you think this is?

Improvise a scene one month after the point where the play ends. What has happened since then? Which characters will be in your improvised scene? How do you want to affect the audience with this scene? Would you consider adding your scene onto the end of your performance of the whole play?

Character Development

1. Write and perform a monologue in reaction to the news of what really happened, in role as Mum, Dad, Simon, George or one of Gretel's friends.

2. Choose a character. Experiment with becoming that character physically. Without speaking, enact how your character sits, walks, dresses to go out, eats, reads a book or magazine and enters a room. Try doing these actions first as yourself, then in role and comment on the differences.

3. Although she says little until the end, the character of Cindy is a demanding one to play. She needs to recede into the group so that we hardly notice her. Yet at the same time, her physical performance should always show her quiet nervousness, shyness and introspection. Find the posture, movement and facial expression suited to Cindy, without overplaying her. Decide how you would play Cindy throughout Scene 14, up to the point where she speaks.

4. Prepare relevant questions with which to 'hot-seat' individual characters. Hot-seating is a rehearsal technique where the performer answers questions in the role of a chosen character. It is important when being hot-seated not to just answer verbally in the way your character would, but to think about body language and how much that communicates to an audience. Consider also how much your character uses eye contact and how much your posture gives away about how you (in role) are really feeling. Is there a difference between what your character *says* and what s/he betrays through body language and mannerisms?

5. Maddy's status as the focal point of her gang is very important. In a group, experiment with treating the performer playing Maddy as though she is royalty. Kneel down in front of her and behave in an exaggerated fashion, like servants! Respond immediately and deferentially to her commands. Choose a scene that Maddy appears in. Prepare five still life tableaux to show five frozen moments from the scene. In each one, Maddy should be the central figure and it should be clear to the audience that she has the highest status in the group. Choose another scene featuring Maddy and her friends. Try rehearsing it with the actor playing Maddy moving freely and spontaneously around the stage, constantly changing direction. The other performers must try to keep up with her whilst also remaining in a group formation around her. Discuss what effect this exercise has on the members of Maddy's gang. Return to performing the scene properly but aim to keep some of the energy of the active version in order to emphasize Maddy's status.

6. Place Maddy on a chair in the middle of the stage with all other performers, in role, grouped around her. Each character should place themselves at a distance which indicates their relationship with or opinion of or attitude towards her. This should also be expressed through body language. Try this with other characters.

7. Scene 3 sets up the characters and dynamics in Gretel's family. Take the first section, up to where George asks, 'Where's Gretel?' Read through, then prepare, a performance of this section using only body language, facial expression, gesture and positioning to communicate to the audience - the situation, how these characters respond to each other and the tensions between them. No speaking

allowed! Think very carefully about how to show Mum being always on edge and nervously anticipating Dad's responses. Think also about how to show the way that Dad is the dominant centre of the scene that everyone else has to revolve around. Try this also with scene 11 from the point where Simon tickles Gretel, through to the end of the scene. There should be a strong contrast in Gretel's body language between the beginning and the end of the scene.

8. Further on in scene 3 Gretel's friends appear for the first time. Apply the same technique to this scene as described above. Aim to communicate what is happening in this scene without using words. Think carefully about grouping and where Cindy is within the group. Facial expression, gesture, posture and physical responses should all communicate anxiety, shock and concern. You can also try reducing the scene down to four tableaux. Then, use the first and last ones as the opening and closing stage pictures when performing the scene properly.

Links

At the beginning of scene 7 Gretel is shown as being metaphorically lost in the forest. (There are references throughout the play to the story of Handsel and Gretel.) Immediately afterwards we see Maddy's gang advancing on Gretel, chanting, 'Nibble, nibble little mouse...' Find this scene and experiment with performing it with the gang circling Gretel as though she is prey. Try it as a sort of variation on the game 'Grandmother's footsteps' with the performers freezing each time Gretel turns around. Make the movements eerie and threatening and try different ways of chanting the lines to create an appropriately menacing and unnerving atmosphere.

Performing the text

1. A performer should never rely only on speaking the text to communicate with the audience. What the audience sees happening is what really brings a performance to life. Often, the spoken parts can be mixed in with long moments of purely visual action. Scene 14 has a lot of talking in order to communicate a lot of information. Rehearse this scene (or sections of it) paying close attention to what each character is doing when not speaking. Consider how best to group everyone and how each individual reacts physically.

2. There are a number of stage directions for silence. Find some and experiment with how long each moment of silence should be – say why.

3. Consider the power of silence as a threat and as a means of creating tension. Experiment with this in Scene 6 with Cindy and Maddy's gang and in the bullying scenes in Scene 7.

Performance notes for Scene 13

In this shadow-play scene, it is important that the audience should assume that they are watching Maddy and Gretel fighting. Maddy is performer 1 (the onlooker), Cindy is performer 2 and Gretel is performer 3. The shadow play can be performed in slow motion and performers should experiment with distances from the screen to distort the images in order to heighten effect. Movement must be choreographed so that at first the audience assumes that performer 2 (Cindy) is Gretel, the victim of the attack. Then, through the means of the two performers swinging each other around, audience focus should shift without their realising to view performer 3 (Gretel) as the victim, because she is the one who falls. Cindy's act of self-defence in pushing Gretel back should make her appear like the aggressor because the previous moments of action have been unclear. Performer 2 should turn away before Gretel falls. There is blackout as soon as Gretel hits the ground.